Dear Parents and Educators,

Welcome to Penguin Young Readers! As parents and educators, you know that each child develops at his or her own pace—in terms of speech, critical thinking, and, of course, reading. Penguin Young Readers recognizes this fact. As a result, each Penguin Young Readers book is assigned a traditional easy-to-read level (1–4) as well as a Guided Reading Level (A–P). Both of these systems will help you choose the right book for your child. Please refer to the back of each book for specific leveling information. Penguin Young Readers features esteemed authors and illustrators, stories about favorite characters, fascinating nonfiction, and more!

Chip Wants a Dog

LEVEL 2

GUIDED READING LEVEL **H**

This book is perfect for a **Progressing Reader** who:
• can figure out unknown words by using picture and context clues;
• can recognize beginning, middle, and ending sounds;
• can make and confirm predictions about what will happen in the text; and
• can distinguish between fiction and nonfiction.

Here are some **activities** you can do during and after reading this book:
• Problem/Solution: The problem in the story is that Chip really wants a dog, but his parents won't let him get one. Discuss the solution in the story and how Chip solves his problem and is no longer lonely.
• Word Repetition: Reread the story and count how many times you read the following words: *dog, if, teach, think, want*. On a separate sheet of paper, work with the child to write a new sentence for each word.

Remember, sharing the love of reading with a child is the best gift you can give!

—Bonnie Bader, EdM
Penguin Young Readers program

*Penguin Young Readers are leveled by independent reviewers applying the standards developed by Irene Fountas and Gay Su Pinnell in *Matching Books to Readers: Using Leveled Books in Guided Reading*, Heinemann, 1999.

PENGUIN YOUNG READERS
Published by the Penguin Group
Penguin Group (USA) LLC, 375 Hudson Street, New York, New York 10014, USA

USA | Canada | UK | Ireland | Australia | New Zealand | India | South Africa | China

penguin.com
A Penguin Random House Company

Library of Congress Cataloging-in-Publication Data is available.

ISBN 978-0-448-48043-5 (pbk)   10 9 8 7 6 5 4 3 2 1
ISBN 978-0-8037-3935-2 (hc)   10 9 8 7 6 5 4 3 2 1

Chip Wants a Dog

by William Wegman

Penguin Young Readers
An Imprint of Penguin Group (USA) LLC

Dogs!

Dogs! Dogs! Dogs!

Chip thinks about dogs.

Chip reads about dogs.

Chip dreams about dogs.

Chip wants a dog!

What would Chip name his dog?

When Chip was a baby,

he wanted a dog.

Dog was the first word he

said.

Without a dog, Chip is lonely.

He does not have anyone

to play with.

If he had a dog,

he would teach it to do tricks.

He would

teach it to sit.

He would

teach it to stay.

He would

teach it to fetch.

He would teach it to roll over.

Good dog!

If Chip had a dog,

it would be his best friend.

But Chip's parents do not

want a dog.

His mother likes cats.

She is a cat person.

Chip's mother does not like

that some dogs shed.

And Chip's father thinks taking care of a dog is hard work. Chip would not have time for his chores.

His parents do not want to talk

about it anymore.

Chip does not understand why he can't have a dog.

All the other kids have dogs.

Before bed, Chip brushes
his teeth.

He looks into the mirror
for a long, long time.

He wonders why he only thinks

about dogs.

That night Chip has a dream.

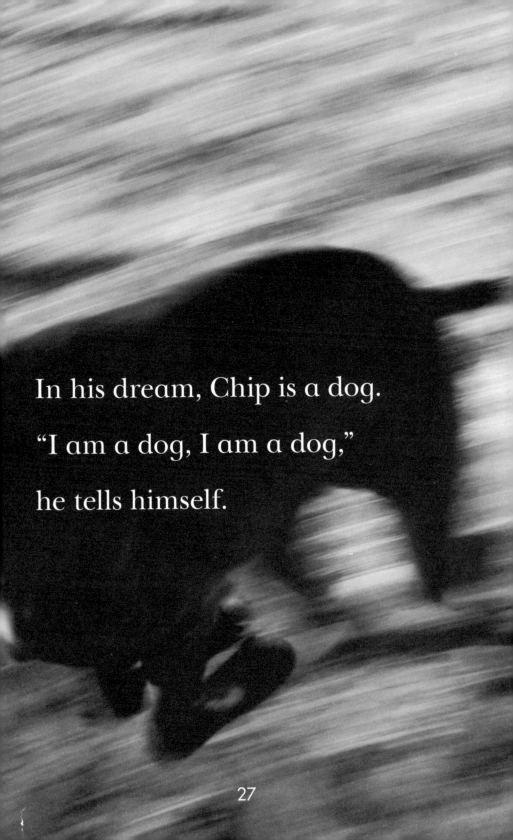

In his dream, Chip is a dog.

"I am a dog, I am a dog,"

he tells himself.

Then Chip wakes up.

Chip does not need a dog.

He *is* a dog!

That day, Chip's life changes.

He now takes himself for a walk.

He teaches himself new tricks.

He gives himself a bone.

Chip makes lots of new friends and is never lonely again!